CENTER COURT
STING

CENTER COURT STING

LITTLE, BROWN AND COMPANY
Books for Young Readers
New York Boston

Little, Brown Books for Young Readers

Hachette Book Group
237 Park Avenue, New York, NY 10017
Visit our Web site at www.lb-kids.com

www.mattchristopher.com

Little, Brown Books for Young Readers is a division of Hachette Book Group, Inc.
The Little, Brown name and logo are trademarks of Hachette Book Group, Inc.

First Paperback Edition: October 1998

Library of Congress Cataloging-in-Publication Data

Christopher, Matthew F.
Center court sting. / Matt Christopher. — 1st ed.
p. cm.
Summary: Daren's tendency to blame everyone but himself when anything goes wrong causes problems with his best friend, with a young neighbor who idolizes him, and with one of his basketball teammates.
ISBN 978-0-316-14278-6 (hc) — ISBN 978-0-316-14205-2 (pb)
[1. Basketball — Fiction. 2. Behavior— Fiction. 3. Self-perception — Fiction.] I. Title.
PZ7.C458Cg 1998 98-16835
[Fic] — dc21

10

COM-MO

Printed in the United States of America

To my great-grandson, Evan Robert

CENTER COURT STING

Daren McCall was *hot*.

It wasn't the noise of the screaming fans in the echoing gym or the glaring lights. It wasn't that the basketball game was close or that he'd been racing up and down the polished hardwood floor for what seemed like hours.

What Daren really was, was *steamed*. He'd expected the game to be a romp. His team, the Rangers, was one of the best in the league, way better than the pathetic Demons, the bunch they were playing.

Daren had hoped to score a lot of points, maybe even a personal high.

But the Demons had hung in all the way. Now, with four minutes left, the Rangers led by just five points, and the game was still up for grabs.

Lou Bettman, the six-foot one-inch Ranger center, was having a terrible game — again. He seemed to be sleepwalking, unable to score or rebound. Daren couldn't understand what had happened to Lou. He was the star of last year's Rangers and had looked even better as this year's season began. Then, suddenly, he'd fallen apart.

But the person who was irritating Daren the most was a guy named Carl Mantell. Carl was guarding Daren. A mediocre player according to his stats, Carl was giving Daren more trouble than Daren had thought he would. No matter what Daren did, Carl stayed in his face, cutting off the lane when he tried to drive or giving him little shoves to keep him off balance. What was worse, the ref, a skinny dude with hair in his eyes, hadn't called these obvious fouls. With a decent ref, Daren felt, Mantell would have fouled out by now.

After Lou blew another layup, the Demons raced up-court. Carl got the ball in the corner and threw a bad shot, way out of his range. The ball bounced hard off the front rim and into the hands of Ranger guard Lynn Mayes, Daren's best friend on the team. Daren, seeing a possible fast break, spun and raced toward the Ranger basket. Lynn's pass was short, making Daren slow down to catch it. As he spun to shoot the hoop, Carl darted in to block him. As Daren threw up an off-balance shot, they collided, and Carl staggered back, arms wheeling. Daren knew he hadn't hit the guy hard and that Carl was acting. Sure enough, the ref blew his whistle. Daren snagged the ball, sure he would be taking a trip to the foul line for two free throws.

A blocking foul on Carl, at last, he thought with satisfaction. But that feeling changed abruptly when he saw the ref pointing at *him.*

"Charging, number four," he said as Daren stared in disbelief. "Green ball."

"*What!*" Daren yelped.

He saw Lynn signal him to cool it, but he was too angry to care. This ref was unreal!

The ref held out his hands. "C'mon, let's have the ball. *Now.*"

Daren slammed the ball to the floor as hard as he could and stomped away. Behind him, he heard another shrill whistle.

"Technical foul, number four!"

Daren's face burned as the crowd booed and jeered. He didn't know if they were booing the ref or him, but he wanted to kick himself for giving the Demons the chance to cut into the Ranger lead. Maybe he could make it up in the last few minutes, if —

"Time out!" shouted Coach Michaels, drilling Daren with an icy glare. As the team went to the sideline, he pointed at Daren.

"Sit," he snapped. "Shawn, go in for Daren. Listen up, everyone." Daren started to protest, but a look at the coach's face made him shut up. The coach began talking to the team as Daren slumped in his seat. He knew that Coach Michaels was mad and that there was no way he'd get back in this game, not even if six Rangers broke their legs.

It wasn't fair. Carl Mantell was playing dirty, the ref was blind, and now the coach was making him look bad by benching him.

When the game resumed, he stared at the floor. He could tell from the crowd's groan that Carl had made the technical. Now the Ranger lead had been cut to four, and the Demons had the ball.

Could the Demons pull this game out? And if they did, would Daren's teammates blame him?

He forced himself to watch. A moment later, he jumped up in excitement when the Rangers intercepted a Demon pass. Guard Cris Campbell banked in a jumper, and Daren cheered. The Ranger lead inched ahead to six points.

A moment later, Mac Gould, the Demon center, took a pass from Carl Mantell, spun away from Lou Bettman, and tried a soft jumper from eight feet. Lou hit Mac's arm as the shot went in. The ref called the foul on Lou, and Gould sank the foul shot. The Ranger lead was cut to three with two minutes left.

Daren slapped his thigh with his lucky

towel. What was going on with Lou? Had he forgotten how to play basketball? Didn't he care anymore? Daren felt like running in and shaking Lou by the shoulders, hard, and yelling at him to wake up. Maybe Daren had not had a very good game, but Lou was totally messing up.

When the Rangers inbounded, the Demons tried to trap Lynn in the backcourt, swarming around him and waving their arms. Shawn Howe came back to help, and Lynn bounced a pass to him. Shawn passed to Cris, who sank another jumper.

The Demons seemed rattled. Lynn intercepted the Demons' inbound pass and laid it in to make the Ranger lead seven. Daren looked at the clock and knew it was all over. The Rangers had the game in their pockets now.

At the final buzzer, the scoreboard read Rangers 52, Demons 45.

The teams headed for the locker rooms. The Demons looked unhappy, but the Rangers weren't too cheerful, either. They knew they hadn't played anywhere near their best.

Daren felt bad about the technical and knew it might have cost his team the game. Just thinking about the events that had led up to it made him hot under the collar. He might have had a good game if Carl Mantell hadn't played dirty and if the ref hadn't needed glasses. It was really their fault he had lost his temper and been benched.

And what was up with that? He was sure that he could have made up for his mistake if the coach hadn't benched him. Coach Michaels should have given him another chance instead of making him look bad.

It just wasn't fair.

The first thing Daren saw in the visitors locker room was the Ranger team manager, Andy Higgins. Andy, with his usual geeky grin, was clapping his hands, trading high fives with whoever was willing, and slapping players on the back. Didn't he see that the Rangers hadn't played well today, even though they'd won?

Apparently, he didn't. "All *right!*" he yelled. "Way to go! Rangers rule!" Andy was no athlete, but he loved basketball and hanging with the Rangers. Daren loved basketball, too, but he doubted he'd spend *his* free time rattling around on an old school bus to away games just to hand out towels and drinks.

"Way to go, Dar!" Andy said, holding out his hand. Daren brushed by him, ignoring the hand. Andy looked hurt, but Daren was too upset to care.

"Right, Andy," called Lou Bettman, sitting by his locker. "Daren did great . . . for the *other* guys. Real smart, Daren, getting a *T*."

Daren heard a couple of others muttering agreement with Lou and felt his temper heat up.

"Hey, Lou," Daren said, sneering. "You want to talk about great games? You want to talk about *my* mistakes? *You* were a real all-star out there — *not*. You couldn't find the basket with a road map, and you wouldn't know what a rebound was if it bit you on the leg. Talk about pathetic. You were the worst —"

Lou stood up quickly and walked away, almost falling over Andy, who was stooping to pick up towels. "Watch it!" he shouted. "Look where you're going!"

"S-sorry, Lou," Andy mumbled as he edged away. "I didn't . . . I mean, I wasn't . . ."

"Hey, McCall! Don't hassle Lou!" Shawn glared at Daren. "Maybe Lou didn't have his shot working, but that doesn't change the fact that what you did was just *stupid*."

Daren knew that Shawn was right. It *had* been stupid. But he wasn't about to admit it, not the way he was feeling. He matched Shawn's glare with one of his own. "That ref was the pits!" he said. "If he hadn't swallowed his whistle, Mantell would've fouled out! First the ref gets on me, and now you! You must be glad I got benched so you could get some playing time. What a team player!"

Shawn looked disgusted. "It's all about you, huh? *You* talk about team players! A *real* team player doesn't blow up like you did, and he doesn't hassle a teammate just because the guy's game was a little off."

"A *little* off!" Daren laughed. Lynn came up behind him and put a hand on his shoulder. Daren shook it off. "Right! And the Grand Canyon's a *little* hole in the ground!"

"Quiet, everybody!" Coach Michaels stood in the doorway and looked around the suddenly silent room.

"That's better," the coach said. "I think you all know we didn't give a hundred percent today. We could just as easily have lost it at the end.

"We play the Blazers next, and you'd better be ready. If you don't pick up your game, those guys will walk all over you. We have our work cut out for us, so be ready to sweat at practice tomorrow. I'll go over the things we need to work on. That's all for now. Daren, come with me."

Uh-oh, Daren thought. As he stood up, Lynn whispered, "Be cool. Hang in there."

In the hallway, Daren faced Coach Michaels but looked away fast. The coach's eyes were cold, and his lips formed a thin line. Daren braced himself to get chewed out.

But the coach didn't say anything at first, and when he did, his voice was soft.

"What happened out there? What did you think you were doing?"

Daren looked up. "I — I guess I sort of blew it, huh?" Daren tried a little smile, but he got no smile in return.

"'Sort of'? You *totally* blew it, big time. Sometimes I wonder what you're thinking."

Daren stopped smiling. "Well, it's just that . . . Coach, didn't you see Mantell shove me around and foul me all game long? That ref was —"

The coach cut Daren off. "So it was all Mantell's and the ref's fault?"

“Well . . .” Daren shrugged. “No, not *all* their fault, but —”

“That technical wasn’t anybody’s fault but yours,” said Coach Michaels. His eyes bored into Daren. “It was that temper of yours — again. We’ve talked about it before.”

Daren looked down. “I know. But —”

“No, Daren. No ‘buts.’ If you can’t learn to control that temper, you’ll wind up hurting the team more than you help it. I won’t have that. Next time you go ballistic in a game, you can expect to spend a lot more time on the bench. Is that clear?”

“Yes, sir,” Daren muttered.

The coach nodded. “All right. Just as long as we understand each other. Now, let’s put it behind us and get ready for the Blazers.”

When Daren went out to the team bus for the trip home, he felt everyone’s eyes on him. He found a seat alone at the back.

"How you doing?" Lynn sat down next to Daren, who shrugged.

Lynn peered at Daren for a moment. "Got chewed out, huh? Well, Coach doesn't hold a grudge. Tomorrow it'll all —"

Daren cut him off. "He doesn't like me. He's going to kick me off the team soon."

Lynn shook his head. "No way, Dar. He likes you as much as he likes any of us. It's just that he —"

Daren hunched forward. "Look, I'd rather be by myself, okay?"

Lynn blinked. Then he shrugged.

"You got it." He moved to another seat, leaving Daren alone.

A few seats ahead, Lou Bettman also sat by himself, staring out the window at nothing.

For a team that had won a game, the trip home was very quiet.

After games, Daren and Lynn usually rode their bikes home together. The ride, and Lynn's easy-going chatter, usually calmed Daren. But today Lynn had a challenge on his hands.

"The Blazers are pretty hot this season," Lynn said, "but we can take them."

"I guess," Daren muttered. "If we don't get that lame ref we had today. Can you believe him? He didn't give me one break!"

"I guess," said Lynn.

Daren stared at his friend. "You *guess?*

Carl did everything but hit me with a baseball bat! If he had, the ref still would've called the foul on me!"

"Well . . ." Lynn pedaled in silence for a moment. "Carl plays tough *D*. In-your-face defense. Against the Blazers, he held Don Spratt to ten points. That's doing a good job, I think."

Daren was amazed. He wanted sympathy, and here his best friend was, praising Carl Mantell! He was practically saying that all the problems today were Daren's fault!

"Carl Mantell plays dirty! End of discussion! If you can't tell the difference between good defense and playing dirty, you should try another sport — like checkers! What kind of friend are you?"

Lynn kept calm, and his voice stayed level. "I'm a good friend. But I don't always have to agree with you. I can say what I think."

"Yeah, well, do me a favor and keep your thoughts to yourself for the rest of the ride," Daren snapped.

Lynn shrugged, and neither one said another word. They parted when Daren pedaled up his driveway and Lynn headed home.

Daren put his bike in the garage and grabbed his backpack from the backseat carrier. As he was closing the garage door, he heard a voice calling him.

"Dar, how'd it go? Did you win?"

His friend and neighbor, twelve-year-old Judy Parnell was smiling at him from her side of the fence between their front lawns. Daren and Judy had known each other since they were babies, and Daren felt his mood improve. He walked over to the fence.

"We won, barely. I didn't do so great."

Judy's smile faded. "That's too bad, but you'll have a great game next time. You never have two bad ones in a row."

Daren smiled for the first time in hours. "Well . . . thanks. I better have, because we're playing the Blazers, and those guys are tough."

"I hope I can come see you. Daren, can I ask you a big favor?"

"No problem. What's up?"

Judy looked back toward her house. "It's about my little brother, Gary."

Gary was eight, and Daren thought he was a nice kid. "What about him?"

"Well, he's really interested in basketball all of a sudden. He watches it on TV, and he's got posters of pro players all over his room. We got him a ball for his birthday, and Dad is going to put up a hoop and backboard in the yard."

Daren nodded. "That's great. It's good for kids to get started young. I was only seven when I got my first ball. My dad and I practiced all the time."

"I remember," Judy said with a smile. "The thing is, my dad is so busy these days that he doesn't have the time right now to help Gary. And Gary needs some coaching. You know, someone to give him tips. I don't know enough about it, so I was hoping that you could help. Gary really looks up to you."

Daren thought a moment. He liked Judy, and he was sure he could get Gary playing well in no time.

"Sure, why not?"

"Oh, that would be so great!" Judy's smile was radiant. "Would you wait a minute, and I'll get Gary. He's doing his homework."

"Sure thing."

Judy ran into her house and came out a moment later with Gary, who had a basketball under his arm. His face lit up at the sight of Daren.

"Hey, Dar!" he yelled. "I got a basketball, see?" He held the ball up.

"That's cool, Gary," Daren said, taking the ball and spinning it on his index finger.

"Gary," said Judy, "would you like Daren to coach you now and then?"

The younger boy's eyes grew round in astonishment. "*Really?* He'd coach *me?*"

"Definitely," said Daren, tossing the ball back to Gary.

"*Awesome!*" Gary caught the ball. "Hey, could we start now?"

Daren laughed. "I can't today. I have homework. But how about tomorrow? I can be here by four-thirty."

"*Yes!*" Gary beamed at Daren and his sister. "Wait'll the guys at school hear!"

Daren reached over the fence and patted Gary's shoulder. "Okay. See you tomorrow afternoon. Bye, Judy!"

"Bye, Daren," she said, "and thanks!"

As Daren walked inside, he realized that his bad mood was gone.

"Hey, Lynn! Wait up!"

Seeing Lynn headed for school the next morning, Daren pedaled hard to catch him. He felt bad about the way he had talked to Lynn the day before and wanted to make sure that everything was all right between them.

"I'm sorry about yesterday," Daren said when he got close. "I don't know why I said those things to you. I was a creep. You're my friend, and you can say whatever you want."

"No problem," Lynn replied with his

usual smile in place. They started toward school.

Daren sighed. "I don't know why I act like that. It's like, I can't stop once I get going. Then, later, I always wish I had kept my mouth shut. You know what I mean?"

Lynn nodded. "Yeah. I just worry that it's going to get you into a big jam someday."

For some reason, Lynn's tone irritated Daren. "Well, we can't all be Mr. Cool, like you," he replied with an edge in his voice.

Lynn gave him a sideways look. "At least you know it's wrong to blow up like that, right?"

Daren shrugged.

"If you *didn't* know," Lynn went on, "then I'd really be worried."

Daren didn't know how to reply to that, so he let the subject drop.

That day at lunchtime, Daren carried his

tray into the cafeteria, with Lynn just behind him. He headed toward a table where some other Rangers players were sitting.

As he neared, Lou Bettman looked up at him. Lou said something to Shawn, who glanced at Daren, then nodded.

Daren hadn't been close enough to hear Lou, but he was certain that Lou was talking about him, and he was ready to bet that it wasn't a compliment. In spite of having promised himself not to lose his temper, he felt himself getting mad. Who did Lou think he was to talk about him?

He and Lynn slid into chairs across the table from Lou and Shawn.

Daren stared at Lou. "Hey, Bettman, what were you saying about me just then?"

"Who says I was talking about you?" Lou snorted. "Maybe I was talking about the weather. Not everything is about you."

Daren unwrapped his sandwich. "Oh, I see. You don't have the guts to say it to my face."

Lou slid his chair back. "You think you know everything, don't you? Well, you don't."

Daren took a bite of his sandwich. When he had swallowed, he said, "So what *were* you saying? Go on — don't be afraid."

Lou stood up quickly. "You think I'm afraid of you, McCall?"

Daren stood, too. "No, you're real brave. Just like you're a great basketball player."

Lou started around the table, but Shawn grabbed his arm, saying, "Don't let him get to you. Don't pay attention to him — he's not worth the trouble."

Meanwhile, Lynn tapped Daren's arm. "What *is* it with you? Listen to yourself, you're doing it *again!*"

"Well, he —," Daren began.

Lynn cut him off. "It's not *him*, it's *you* — and you better cut it out."

Shawn had his arm around Lou's shoulders. "Let's get out of here." As the two walked away, Shawn turned and glared at Daren. "You're a real pain, you know?"

Daren glared back. When Lou and Shawn had disappeared, he picked up his sandwich again. But he wasn't hungry. Lynn finished his own lunch in silence, picked up his trash, and left Daren sitting alone for the rest of the period.

After his last class of the day, Daren was on his way to the locker room when he saw Shawn Howe by the door. Shawn walked over.

"I want to talk to you."

Daren stood still. "Yeah?"

"Leave Lou alone, okay? You're always giving him a hard time, taking shots at him every day. Why don't you cut it out?"

"Are you his bodyguard?" Daren asked. "If he has a problem, let him tell me himself."

He started to walk around Shawn, but Shawn got in his way. "I'm not his bodyguard. I'm his friend. And I'm telling you because he won't. Get off his back, all right?"

Daren looked Shawn up and down, slowly. "And what if I don't?"

"If you don't," said Shawn darkly, "I —"

Suddenly they heard angry voices in the locker room. One voice was Lou's. The boys went to see, and found Lou yelling at Andy.

"That's a stupid place to leave an open can of paint! What's wrong with you? Is your brain out for repair?"

Andy flushed. "That's not fair. I just left it there for a second —"

Seeing Shawn and Daren, Lou pointed to an open can of red poster paint on the floor. "He leaves that paint sitting there where anyone could knock it over! I almost tripped on it!"

Andy picked up the can. "I only left it there for a second, while I —"

"You shouldn't leave it there at all!" yelled Lou. "You're here to *help* us, not booby-trap us!"

Andy's eyes flashed. "I didn't —"

"What's going on here?" Coach Michaels stood in the doorway to his office. "What's the problem? Why all the shouting?"

Lou pointed to Andy. "He left an open can of paint in the middle of the floor!"

"I had to get towels," Andy said. "I was gone for just a second."

"All right, enough," said the coach. He looked at both boys. "Let's get ready to practice. Shake hands, you two."

Lou scowled but shook Andy's hand. Neither of the two looked happy.

As Coach Michaels had promised, the

Rangers had a tough practice, running set plays over and over. At one point, Shawn grabbed a rebound and pivoted, the ball held high. As he spun around, his elbow slammed into Daren's face. Daren stumbled back, rubbing his jaw.

"Sorry," said Shawn, not sounding sorry.

"You did that on purpose!" said Daren.

"Hey, I didn't see you!" insisted Shawn.

Daren's jaw ached. "Yeah, right."

"I saw what happened," said Lou. "It was an accident, and you know it, McCall."

"Accident! Right! Look who's talking, Mr. Basketball himself! Hey, Bettman is it true that 'Lou' is short for 'loser'?"

Shawn shoved Daren, hard. "I told you to cut that stuff out!"

The Coach's whistle sounded loudly. "Hold it! What is the matter with you guys lately?" He stared around at the team, his hands on his hips. No one spoke.

"Look," said the coach. "If you people want to fight each other, fine. Go out for the wrestling team. But if you want to play basketball, this has to stop. *Now*. If you hope to beat the Blazers, you'll need all your energy for that."

He paused to look at Shawn and Daren, who couldn't meet his eyes. He shook his head and took a deep breath.

"Daren, go get an ice pack for your jaw." Daren opened his mouth to say he was fine, but the coach's eyes told him he'd better go whether he needed it or not.

He stalked into the locker room and found the first-aid kit in the bathroom. Still fuming, he pulled out the ice pack, crushed the inner bag of chemicals, then held the rapidly cooling plastic bag to his face. As he did so, he caught sight of himself in the mirror. The look of anger on his face startled him, and he dropped his eyes. As his jaw numbed with the cold, he willed his temper to cool, too. Five minutes later, he tossed the pack into the trash and returned to the court.

The rest of the practice was uneventful. At the end, the coach called everyone to the sidelines.

"That's it for today. See you tomorrow — and you'd better be thinking about basketball and your next game, not wrestling one another."

The players started for the locker room. "Daren," the coach called out. "Come here."

Coach Michaels walked Daren over to a bench by the court and sat down.

"How's the jaw?" asked the coach once the other players had gone.

"Okay," Daren answered. "A little sore."

"I saw what happened, and I know it wasn't

all your doing," he said. "But I want you to understand this: When you get on a player like you've done with Lou lately, it not only hurts that player, but it also hurts the whole team. It also makes for bad feelings among other players.

"It has to stop. I'd like you to knock off the nasty remarks. Can you do that?"

Daren wanted to defend himself, but he knew it would be a bad idea. So he simply nodded. "Okay, I promise."

"All right, Daren. I think that it would be a good thing if the Rangers can all start pulling together from here on in, because —"

"*McCall!* Is this your idea of a joke?"

Lou Bettman had come back to the gym with an angry scowl on his face and a pair of street shoes in his hand.

The shoes were bright red!

"What happened?" asked the coach.

Lou held the shoes up for the coach to inspect. "Look at this! Someone took that paint in the locker room and painted them red!"

Coach Michaels took the shoes and looked at them closely. "When did this happen?"

Lou pointed at Daren. "Ask him! He'd be the one to know! He did it!"

Daren couldn't believe it. Lou was accusing *him!* True, he and Lou weren't exactly buddies, but this was *unbelievable!*

Daren was stunned to see the coach look at him suspiciously. Did *he* believe it, too?

Daren opened his mouth to speak, but he didn't know what to say.

"See?" yelled Lou. "He can't deny it!"

Finally, Daren found his voice. "That's totally bogus. I didn't touch those shoes."

The coach dabbed up some paint that had dripped onto the bench. "The paint's still wet," he said. "It happened a little while ago."

Lou nodded. "Sure! When Daren went into the locker room, *that's* when it happened."

The coach frowned.

"And you saw Andy's paint," Lou continued angrily, "and you opened my locker —"

"I did not! That's a lie!"

Lou turned to Coach Michaels. "It *was* him. Who else would do it?"

Daren shook his head. "It wasn't me."

The coach held up his hands. "All right, stop yelling, both of you. Lou, you can't just assume Daren did it. You have no proof. Wear your basketball shoes, and I'll see about getting these cleaned." Lou started to protest, but the coach shook his head. "Go home, Lou. Now."

Lou stomped away. Coach Michaels looked at Daren for a minute, saying nothing.

"I *didn't do it!*" Daren could hardly talk, he was so upset. "I *didn't!*"

"Okay, Daren. I'll take your word for it."

Daren opened his mouth to protest his innocence again. Coach Michaels cut him off.

"*But,*" he said, "there's a reason Lou suspects you. Think about what it is."

Daren scowled. "He just doesn't like me."

Coach Michaels cocked an eyebrow. "Doesn't like you, huh? Now, why wouldn't Lou like a nice, friendly guy like you?"

"I don't know!" The coach's eyebrow raised higher. Daren sighed. "Well . . . I guess, because I sometimes bad-mouth him."

"'Sometimes'? How about all the time? Lately, you never stop. That's what I was talking about. I was hoping you could tell me *why*."

Daren thought for a moment. "Well, he . . . he's been playing really badly and letting us down. He's hurting the team."

"If a teammate is having a rough time," the coach said, "then you try to encourage him and make him feel better — you *don't* make him feel like a jerk. That's something about being on a team that you don't seem to have learned yet."

Daren didn't see why he should compliment a player who was hurting the team, but he knew better than to say so.

The coach sighed. "Okay, Daren, I believe you didn't paint those shoes. I also know that if you give people a hard time, they'll think the worst of you. Give that some thought."

Daren felt like asking the coach why he wasn't coming down on Lou for giving *him* a hard time but only said, "Yes, sir. I will."

Coach Michaels finally smiled. "All right, then. See you tomorrow for practice."

Lynn and most of the other players had left already when Daren entered the locker room. But that was fine with Daren. Even if the coach believed he hadn't pulled that dumb stunt with Lou's shoes, most of the other Rangers probably thought he was the culprit. Lou was sure to have laid the blame on him. Maybe even Lynn thought so. Why else would Lynn not have waited to ride home with him?

As he rode up his driveway, Daren heard his name called. He saw Gary Parnell standing by his driveway, his basketball under one arm and brand-new, fancy-looking sneakers on his feet.

"Hi, Daren! I got new shoes!" Gary's eyes were bright with excitement, and he wore a big, happy grin.

Daren had forgotten about his agreement to help Judy's little brother learn basketball, and he definitely didn't feel like doing it — not now, at least. But he didn't feel much like going in and facing his parents' questions about practice, either. So he put away his bike and joined Gary in the Parnells' yard.

Gary's dad had put up a backboard and basket over their garage door. Gary waited, bouncing the ball awkwardly on the driveway pavement, as Daren approached.

"Can you show me how to do a jump shot?" asked Gary.

Daren shook his head. "Let's start with something simpler. Something important, though."

Gary looked a little disappointed, but he smiled and nodded. "Sure, Daren."

"Okay," Daren said, trying to forget his bad mood. "Let's work on dribbling, okay?"

"Dribbling?" Gary's face fell. "I already know how to dribble. Look!"

He bounced the ball hard off the pavement, staring at it the whole time. After a few bounces, it hit his foot and bounced into the bushes by the house. Gary ran after it, returned with the ball, and started bouncing it again, never letting his eyes leave the ball.

"See?" he said. "I dribble pretty good."

"Actually, you're doing it wrong. You don't want to watch the ball while you dribble. If your eyes are always on the ball, you can't see the court," Daren pointed out. "You can't see where anyone else is, either, on your team or the other team. You have to dribble without watching. Here, I'll show you."

He snatched Gary's ball away in mid-bounce and started dribbling it, his eyes on Gary the whole time. He switched from right hand to left and back. He started with high, slow bounces, then speeded up, never looking at the ball.

"See? I'm watching the court and the

other players while I dribble. Otherwise, I won't know when to pass or whether some guy is going to try to steal the ball away from me."

He turned away from Gary so that his body shielded the ball from the youngster. With one swift move, he pivoted, drove past Gary, and banked a soft layup off the backboard and through the hoop.

"Wow! That was neat!" Gary stared at Daren in awe. "Let me try!"

He bounced the basketball a few times, but his eyes stayed on the ball, and the third bounce went off his leg, straight to Daren.

Daren grabbed the ball. "Whoa! Take it easy, kid. There's a difference between bouncing a basketball and dribbling it. Right now, you're just bouncing the ball."

He started bouncing the ball hard with his arm stiff and his palm flat.

"See?" said Daren. "That's you."

Gary blushed.

"Your hand is flat, like a Ping-Pong paddle. *This* is dribbling."

Daren relaxed, his knees flexed, looking at Gary again.

"See?" he asked as he dribbled. "Look at my hands. See how my fingers are bent? They're controlling the ball. And I don't move my arm a lot when I dribble. My wrist does most of the work. You were doing this." Daren began to slap at the ball with his arm and wrist straight. He made it look as awkward as he could.

Daren tossed the ball to Gary, who looked nervous. "Use your fingers more, instead of the palm of your hand. Okay?"

"Uh-huh," Gary said, and began to bounce the ball again. He bounced it hard, and on the second bounce, the ball came up hard and bent his index finger back.

"*Ow!*" he yelled, shaking his hand. "That hurt!"

"What are you bouncing the ball so hard for?" Daren asked, smirking. "You trying to kill worms? Try again. Easier this time."

Gary nodded slowly as he took the ball. He chewed on his lower lip, then with a deep breath, he tried to dribble. He got the ball bouncing well, but he kept looking at the ball.

Daren darted forward and stole the ball away. "What did I just tell you?" he demanded. "*Don't* look at the ball! Do it again, and keep your eyes on me this time."

He flipped the ball to Gary. The younger boy's eyes were shiny, and he blinked rapidly. But he took the ball again and started bouncing it. He kept his eyes on Daren. The third bounce hit the edge of the driveway and flew into the bushes. Gary stared at Daren, who shook his head sadly.

"Great. I'm not sure if you're going to learn to dribble first or kill the bushes in front of your house."

Gary's lower lip trembled. He turned, ran to his front door, yanked it open, and vanished inside. The door slammed.

Daren stared after him, shrugged, and went home. He had tried, but as far as he could see, Gary was not, and would never be, a basketball player.

He was working on his English homework a few minutes later when the phone in his room rang. It was Judy Parnell, and even over the phone, Daren could hear that she was mad.

"What happened with you and Gary?"

"Huh?" asked Daren. "I tried to give him a lesson, but it didn't work out. Why?"

"Gary's in his room, crying," Judy said. "He won't talk to me. What did you do to him?"

Daren felt angry. That's what happens, he thought, when you do someone a favor. "I didn't do *anything* to him! I told him what to do, and he didn't do it. I told him again, and he still didn't do it, and then he gave up and ran away."

"I should have known better," Judy said. "It's my fault."

"What are you talking about?"

"Gary is eight years old," Judy said, with ice in her voice. "Eight-year-olds aren't usually great athletes yet. They have small hands, and they can't use them like bigger kids. Older kids ought to know that.

"I don't know exactly what you said, but Gary looked up to you, and you really hurt his feelings. I hope you're satisfied. Thanks a lot!"

There was a loud *bang* in Daren's ear as Judy slammed down the phone.

Daren hung up and lay down on his bed, staring up at the ceiling.

Why was everybody giving him a hard time? It wasn't his fault the kid couldn't play basketball, but Judy, just like everyone else today, had to point the finger at him!

"We can beat these guys," said Coach Michaels to the Rangers sitting around him in the locker room. The game would start in a few minutes. "But against the Blazers, we have to play our best defense. Keep your heads in the game, and help one another on the court! Their big threat is Don Spratt. He can hit outside or get loose inside. Daren will guard him, but give him help. Try to keep Spratt under wraps."

"Right," Lou Bettman whispered just loud enough for Daren to hear. "Daren needs all the help he can get."

Daren heard him but kept quiet. With the threat of being benched hanging over his head, he was trying to do what the coach wanted and hadn't hassled Lou in days. Lou didn't seem to care.

"Okay," said the coach. "Take a minute, and think about what you have to do." He walked into his office.

Once he was gone, Daren stood to warm up his legs. But he stopped in mid-stretch when he heard an angry voice snap, "Lay off Daren, Lou. Keep your mind on the game."

Daren was surprised to recognize the voice as Lynn's. Lynn, who never lost his temper!

Shawn Howe jumped up to face Lynn. "Mind your own business," he said. "Daren's been on Lou's case all season."

Lynn took a step toward Shawn. "Guess you'd rather rag on Daren than win this game, huh? Real smart, Howe."

"Will you cut it out?" demanded Peter

Stuber, a Ranger reserve guard. "Give it a rest, okay? We're sick of it. *I* am, anyway."

That shut everyone up. Daren gave Lynn a "thanks anyway" look, then went to his locker for his lucky towel. He'd had the old towel, with his initials written on it in marking pen, for years. He kept it next to him on the bench during every game. Usually it was in his locker before a game, but today it wasn't anywhere to be seen.

"Andy!" Daren yelled. "Yo, *Higgins!*"

The manager's face peered out from behind a row of lockers. "Yeah?"

"Where's my lucky towel?" Daren demanded.

Andy stared at him. "Isn't it there?"

Daren rolled his eyes. "If it was *here,* would I ask you where it was, Sherlock?"

"Uh . . . I guess not . . ." Andy blinked and looked around. "I don't know, Daren. Sorry."

"Wonderful," Daren said. "Great, Andy. All

you have to do is take care of the towels, and you can't even do *that* right."

"That's not so! I have lots of stuff to —"

"Oh, forget it." Daren turned away in disgust, leaving Andy standing there.

Coach Michaels came out of his office. "Okay, Rangers, let's go." He led the team onto the gym floor, where they got a cheer from their home fans. As they warmed up, Daren tried not to think about the missing lucky towel.

During the early part of the game, Daren didn't need luck. He had the hot hand, and Lynn found him and snapped sharp, accurate passes in his direction. On the few times Daren missed the basket, Lou boxed out the Blazer center, Toby Flynn, and hit the rebound. Lou was looking more like his old self, controlling the boards, and the Rangers were tough — at least on offense.

But the Blazers were also scoring. Don

Spratt was quick — so quick that Daren's shorter legs simply couldn't keep up.

To make things more difficult, the Blazers were the best passers that Daren had ever played against. They had the ball all over the place, using bounce passes, crisp chest passes, and even the occasional long bomb. All the while, Spratt dodged and feinted, moving in and out and across the key. When Spratt got loose, as he did almost every time the Blazers were on offense, a teammate would get him the ball and he'd lay it up or sink a high-arching jump shot.

Daren was frustrated. Try as he might, he always seemed to be one step behind Spratt. His frustration mounted when Coach Michaels put Shawn in to try to do better. Shawn was taller than Daren, but not as quick, and Spratt kept scoring. Shawn picked up three fouls right away and had to come out.

Back on the court, Daren vowed to do

better. On their first offensive move down the court, he sneaked inside on the baseline. Cris Campbell saw him and fired a perfect bounce pass past the Blazer defenders. Daren moved to put it up right away. But just as he released the ball, he saw Don Spratt take off for the other basket, which distracted him for just a fraction of a second. His shot missed. Bucky Manning, the Blazer point guard, snagged the rebound and threw a long baseball-type pass to Spratt, who was all alone underneath to score.

At halftime, Daren was gasping, and the Blazers had a two-point lead. Daren couldn't remember ever working harder in a game. Though he had some points, Spratt had scored more. Just as the coach had anticipated, it was going to take more than one player to keep Spratt in check.

Daren walked by Lou, who was slumped

in front of his locker, wiping his face with a towel, then stopped.

"Why don't you double-team Spratt?" Daren snapped. "Coach said to help on defense. If you would block his driving lane, he wouldn't —"

"Is it *my* fault *your* man is scoring? I have my own man to guard," Lou answered. "Don't blame me!"

Daren sneered. "You don't care if we win or lose, just so I'm the one who looks bad. Right?"

"Are you two at it again?" a voice barked behind them. Daren and Lou looked up and saw Coach Michaels, a hard look on his face. "Team meeting. Now. And leave your argument behind."

Coach Michaels whistled sharply to quiet the rest of his players. "I don't have to tell you that Don Spratt is doing most of the damage so far," he said. He shot a look at Lou. "And let's get something clear: I don't want anyone blaming Daren. Spratt does this to every team in the league. He's good at getting free to shoot — it's that simple. But we need to stop him to win today, and here's a way we could do it."

Using the chalkboard, the coach showed how the Rangers needed to collapse on Spratt, hemming him in and making it tough for the Blazers to get him the ball. Coach Michaels explained that Daren's job in the second half would be to stay between Spratt and the basket, while the other Rangers would stay between Spratt and the ball, wherever it was on the court. Maybe that would slow down the star forward and let the Rangers get control of the game.

"Rangers, huddle up." All the Rangers formed a circle and stuck a hand into the middle. The coach placed his hands on top. "This is our game to win. If we play like a team, we *will* win! Make these guys earn their points! Remember, defend with your legs as well as your arms! I don't want to see you waving your arms as a Blazer goes by you. You have to keep moving, block the lanes, know where the ball is, and keep your heads in the game! Ready to get 'em?"

"Yeah!" they shouted in chorus.

The coach clapped. "All right! Let's go!"

As the second half began, the coach's strategy looked good. The Blazers tried to force passes to Spratt, but the Rangers picked them off and turned the interceptions into baskets, giving themselves a two-point lead. The Blazer coach jumped up and called time out.

"All right!" said Coach Michaels on the sideline. "Tough *D!* They're out of sync!"

But in the time-out, the Blazers made changes of their own. On their next possession, Blazer guard Bucky Manning took advantage of the fact that the Rangers were clustered around Don Spratt and not guarding their own men closely. With no one on him, the little guard hit a jumper from behind the foul line to tie the game.

On the following Ranger possession, Lynn got the ball to Lou. Lou missed a close shot that Blazer Toby Flynn rebounded. This time, Lynn picked Bucky up outside and stayed on top of him. But Bucky faked left, drove to his right around Lynn, and hit a layup.

The Rangers put the ball in play. Lynn passed to Lou under the basket. Instead of shooting or passing, Lou tried to get closer to the basket — and was called for walking. Bucky tossed the inbounds pass to Toby Flynn, who gave it back. Manning raced down the court and, when Lynn came up to head him off, fired a bullet pass to Don Spratt. With Daren in his face, Spratt wheeled and made a beautiful hook shot. Two more points! The Blazers were ahead by four.

It seemed like whatever the Rangers tried to do, the Blazers stayed one step ahead of them. When they concentrated on Spratt, Bucky Manning took over, hitting from outside, driving, or getting the ball to Toby Flynn under the basket. If they eased up on Don and spread their defense out, Bucky would find the tall forward with a sharp pass.

Lou looked like his feet were weighed down with cement. He stopped getting rebounds, and Toby Flynn, who wasn't much of a shooter, got a few baskets. Daren cooled off in the second half and couldn't seem to hit anything at all.

Only Lynn's play kept the game from becoming a total disaster. He was all over the floor, stealing passes, scoring, and making assists. Daren thought that Lynn had never looked better — but it was in a losing cause.

Even with Lynn's heroics, the Rangers trailed by twelve with five minutes left. Don Spratt took a pass from Bucky and whirled to shoot. Daren jumped with him, right arm extended. He deflected the shot, touching nothing but ball. When the ref blew his whistle, Daren spun around to stare in disbelief.

"Number four, defense — on the arm," said the ref. "Two shots."

Before Daren could scream, Lynn grabbed him. "Dar, chill! No technicals!"

Daren let his breath out and nodded to Lynn, who smiled. "You're my man," Lynn said.

"Yeah," Daren said. But he was mad. He knew that he had been robbed again.

Don Spratt made the free throws, and Coach Michaels called time out.

"It's not over yet," he reminded his team. "There's time for us to get back into it. One or two quick baskets could still turn it around. The main thing is not to give up or lose your composure. Just play your game."

But Daren felt that the Rangers were beaten. They weren't together. He had lost his touch, Lou was sleepwalking, and nobody could stop the Blazer scoring machine. It wasn't their day. Lynn couldn't beat these guys all by himself. The crowd, which had cheered loudly for the Rangers most of the game, grew quiet, and some people got up to leave. They, too, seemed to know that there would be no miracle comeback.

With three minutes to go, the Blazer coach took out his starters and cleared his bench. They were up by eighteen, and he wanted the subs to get some playing time.

Against the subs, the Rangers cut into the lead. At the final buzzer, the Blazer margin of victory was eleven. But the Rangers knew it hadn't really been that close. They had been blown out — and on their home court, too.

Daren walked off the floor with the silent Rangers. He hated to lose any game, but this one was especially embarrassing. Shaking his head, he walked toward his locker — and stopped short, staring in shock.

Taped to his locker door was a towel —

his lucky towel. But he almost didn't recognize it because it was smeared with red paint. A sign with red lettering was pinned to it.

It said, IT TAKES MORE THAN LUCK TO BE A DECENT PLAYER. MAYBE YOU SHOULD STICK TO USING A PAINTBRUSH INSTEAD OF A BASKETBALL.

Daren ripped the towel off the door and marched toward Lou, who was sitting by his locker. He threw the towel on the floor in front of him.

"You think this is funny?" he yelled.

Lou looked at the towel and then back at Daren. "What are you talking about?" he asked, with a puzzled expression.

"You know what I'm talking about!" Daren kicked the towel down the aisle. "Is this how you get back at me for painting those shoes — which I didn't do, anyway?"

Lynn hurried over. "What's going on?" he asked.

Daren picked up the towel, waved it at Lynn, and read the message out loud. "I found this hanging on my locker! It's Lou's idea of a joke!"

Lynn looked at Lou, who shook his head. "Hey, *I* didn't do it. Don't look at *me!*"

Daren laughed. "Yeah, sure! I know you've had it in for me for a long time, and —"

"*I've* had it in for *you!*" Lou looked amazed. "You've been on my case for weeks! You never miss a chance to take a shot at me! And then you ruined a good pair of shoes —"

"I told you, *I didn't do that!*" Daren was raging. "And I only ride you when you screw up in a game. Which is, like, all the time!"

Lynn tried to get between Daren and Lou, but Daren pushed him aside.

Shawn ran up. "I told you to cut it out," he said to Daren.

"Shawn's right," said Peter Stuber at his locker. "Daren runs his mouth too much, and not just at Lou. I mean, he's not Michael Jordan!"

"Lou played bad today," Cris snapped, getting in on the quarrel. "We all know it. He's been terrible for a long time now!"

Suddenly every Ranger was yelling, some defending Lou and some taking Daren's side. A few just wanted everyone to shut up and chill. Voices got louder, and feelings got uglier.

The coach came out of his office, looked at the yelling players, and shouted, *"Listen up, all of you! QUIET!!"*

The noise stopped. Coach Michaels sighed and began pacing back and forth. "I don't get it," he said quietly. "I really don't."

Daren felt his anger dissolve. The other Rangers seemed to feel the same way.

The coach went on softly, as if he didn't have the energy to yell anymore. "At the start of the season, we had a shot at the title. Now, today, we got blown out — not because the Blazers are so much better, but because they *played* better. They moved the ball and played team *D*. They knew what to do and did it.

"Now here you are, yelling at each other." He saw the towel by Daren's locker, picked it up, and read the message. He sighed.

"We play the Rebels next, the team with the best record in the league. They have Drew Capp, who's six-foot-two and owns the boards. They have Tony Tisdale, the league's top scorer. If you can't get it together, we may as well not bother to show up."

No one spoke. "Lou, Daren, stay here,"

said the coach. "You others, get some rest."

Lynn nudged Daren. "See you outside."

Daren nodded. He saw Shawn speak to Lou, who shook his head angrily. Shawn whispered more, but Lou said, *"No!"*

"Guys," the coach said, "in my office."

Shawn walked away, looking unhappy.

The players took seats, and the coach sat on a corner of his desk. "I try not to get mixed up in your off-court lives. But when it hurts the team, I want to clear it up. Talk to me."

"Well, I didn't put that thing on Daren's locker, no matter what he says," Lou insisted.

"I didn't paint those shoes," said Daren. "I may talk a lot, but I wouldn't mess up someone's stuff. No matter what *he* says."

"Okay," Coach Michaels said. "So, neither of you did anything to each other. Can you agree and put this behind us?"

Lou frowned. "Well . . ."

Daren shrugged. "I don't know . . ."

The coach stood. "Daren, wait outside for a moment."

Daren left the office, certain that Lou still blamed him for the shoes. Just as he *knew* that Lou had ruined his lucky towel. Who else would do it?

A minute later, Lou came out of the office and left without speaking.

Coach Michaels poked his head through the office door and beckoned.

"Like I said before, I don't think you painted those shoes," he said. Daren smiled. "*And* I don't think Lou trashed your towel. It's not like him."

"But he must have!" Daren protested.

"Funny, Lou said the same about you just now," said the coach. "But that's not the main problem here. I've coached for a long time. I've had great teams and not-great teams. But no team ever let grudges hurt their game. I don't know what to do. I'm stumped."

"It's not all *my* fault," Daren exclaimed.

"No," the coach agreed. "But — now hear me out, and don't get angry — you have a way of saying hurtful things, Daren. Maybe you don't even know how much they hurt, but they do. You definitely tend to throw fuel on the fire."

Daren felt resentful. Coach Michaels was blaming all the team's problems on him!

"I can see by the look on your face that you think I'm out to get you," the coach went on. "But I'm not. *No one* is. But I want you to try to see what can happen when you're always putting people down. They remember and may look for payback. Then maybe a friend of yours decides to get *that* person back, and one little incident snowballs.

"When I talk to you about it, you get this

look, like you're being made the fall guy. The bottom line is, you have to learn to control your temper and not say hurtful things. I'm your coach, and I thought that meant something. But maybe it doesn't, because I don't seem to be able to get through to you."

"But —," Daren began. The coach held up a hand.

"I don't want to hear explanations of why it's not your fault." Coach Michaels folded his arms. "I hate to say this, Daren, but I don't feel I have a choice. If you can't control your moods and outbursts, right away, I'll do one of two things: Either I'll bench you and use you as a sub, or I'll have to take you off the team altogether."

Lynn was waiting for Daren outside. "How was it?" asked Lynn. "What'd he say?"

Daren didn't speak. He was afraid that, if he tried, he might start crying. A million feelings whirled in his head. Everyone was blaming him, but he hadn't done anything wrong. Well, not enough for him to be kicked off the team!

Riding home, Lynn broke the silence. "Dar? I'm your friend. I want to help."

Daren looked at Lynn. "Yeah? Then you're the only one. Everyone else hates me, even the coach. He wants me off the Rangers."

"He — you sure? It's not his style to —"

"He *said* so!" Daren braked to a squealing stop. "He wants me out! Maybe I'll quit and save him the trouble! The team would probably throw a party, and *you'd* probably go!"

Lynn stopped and faced Daren. "Did he say, 'I'm kicking you off' or 'If you don't get your act together, I may have to kick you off'?"

"What's the difference?" A voice in Daren's head said *chill*, but he couldn't stop himself. "He blames *me!* So do you, don't you?"

Lynn stared at Daren. "I —"

"Don't you?" screamed Daren.

"Get a grip," snapped Lynn, finally angry. "Listen to me! You say mean things, and when someone else does it, too, you complain! 'It's not my fault!' Here's a bulletin — some of it *is* your fault! And, I *am* your friend! I'm trying to make you see how you hurt yourself."

"You're even dumber than you look! Who needs that kind of friend? *I* sure don't!"

Lynn spun around and pedaled away. Daren suddenly felt awful and called to Lynn, but the other boy vanished around the corner. Daren slowly headed home. Now he had gone and done it. Now he really had no friends at all.

But Lynn wouldn't back him up. He blamed Daren, like everyone else.

Still . . . Lynn *had* defended him in the past and could make Daren feel good when he was down about something. They'd been buddies since kindergarten. Now Lynn would never talk to him or hang with him, ever again.

By the time Daren reached home, he was feeling as bad as he had ever felt in his life.

As he got off his bike, Daren saw Gary Parnell sitting on his porch, looking as unhappy as Daren felt. The boy didn't have his basketball.

Daren decided he might feel better if he offered Gary a lesson. He walked over, but Gary paid no attention until he spoke.

"Hey, want another lesson? We could —"

Gary got up and walked into his yard.

Daren stared, not sure if he should go after him and ask again.

At that moment, Judy Parnell appeared.

"Hi," said Daren, hoping that Judy's anger had been forgotten.

Judy did not smile back. "What do you want?" Her voice, like her face, was unfriendly.

"I — I thought maybe Gary wanted some more basketball tips, so I asked him, but he just walked away."

"I told you," answered Judy. "He doesn't want to play basketball anymore. He says he *hates* it. He tried to throw his ball away, but I took it out of the garbage and put it away, in case he changes his mind. Maybe he will, if you leave him alone."

"*Me?*" Daren felt like the wind had been knocked out of him. "What did *I* do?"

"You don't have a clue?" Judy shook her head. "You were Gary's hero. He was so excited that you were going to help him, he couldn't stop talking about it.

"But when you were here yesterday, it was like you were a different person. Gary told me — once he stopped crying, that is. You said these horrible things, and imitated him, and everything. You made him feel totally dumb and useless."

Daren tried to defend himself. "All I did was try to show him how to dribble, and he wouldn't do what I said — that's all. Maybe I was a little hard on him, but —"

"'A *little* hard'? Amazing!" Judy turned to

walk away, then turned to face Daren again. "You really don't understand, do you? You don't see how you hurt Gary and made him feel awful with your nasty remarks. I wouldn't have believed it, but it's true. That's kind of sad."

Daren didn't know what to say. "I — I didn't — I never — it wasn't —"

Judy's eyes flashed in anger. "Oh no, *don't you dare* say that it wasn't your fault! The best thing for you to do now is to stay away from Gary. You've hurt him enough."

"Okay," Daren muttered.

"And I'd like you to stay away from me, too." With that, Judy turned, walked into her house, and shut the door.

Daren slammed the door behind him. His dad called from the basement, where he was in his workshop, but Daren didn't feel like talking. Taking the stairs two at a time, he ducked into his room and flopped onto his bed.

He stared at the ceiling. Maybe he could just lie there for a month or two. He didn't know what to do now. Lynn never got angry with him. Judy and he had always been friendly. Now even they didn't want to be friends.

Was what they were saying true? He knew his temper got out of control sometimes, but did what he say make such a huge impact?

Daren didn't know.

He lay there for a while. The ceiling didn't have answers, but at least it didn't blame him for anything. That was an improvement.

A little later, Daren heard a knock on his door. It opened slowly, and his father peered in.

"Hey, champ, how you doing?"

Daren didn't look over. "Okay, I guess." He hoped his dad would leave him alone.

"Okay?" Mr. McCall pulled over Daren's desk chair and sat facing the bed. "I have to admit, you don't *look* too okay to me. You look kind of down. If you're really okay, fine. But if something's bothering you, I wish you'd tell me. It might make you feel better to talk about it."

Daren rolled on his side and propped his head on his hand, facing his father.

"I don't know," he said, after thinking for a moment. "I don't know what's going on. The other guys on the Rangers don't like me. Even Lynn is mad at me. Coach Michaels told me he may kick me off the team —"

Daren's dad frowned. "The coach said that? That's surprising."

Daren nodded. "Now even Judy doesn't want to talk to me. It isn't fair! What'd *I* do?"

Daren collapsed onto his back again.

"Yes," said Mr. McCall. "I heard about a problem with Judy — and her little brother."

"I was explaining how to dribble!" said Daren. "He wanted help, so I was helping him, but he ran away and Judy won't talk to me."

Mr. McCall looked serious. "So I heard. You've been friends since you could walk."

He was quiet for a long moment, then suddenly chuckled.

"What's so funny?" Daren asked.

"I'm not laughing at what happened between you and Judy. I was thinking of when *I* started teaching *you* basketball. Remember?"

"Yeah," said Daren. "I was pretty little."

"You were seven," said Mr. McCall. "A year younger than Gary is. And, as I remember, you weren't very good at it."

"I was only seven!"

"Right," agreed his father. "You weren't strong enough to reach the basket. You'd throw the ball hard as you could, and it would be four feet short of the rim! I wish I'd had a video camera. It was pretty funny."

"Uh-huh." Daren wondered if his dad was making fun of him.

Mr. McCall leaned forward. "But you were

doing the best you could. So I'd just say, 'Way to go!' I knew you'd get better when you got older. And that's what happened."

"Well . . . yeah," Daren said slowly.

"Now, imagine you're seven. You throw the ball, and it goes up two feet and hits the garage door. And I laugh at you, or I say, 'Guess I'll have to raise the driveway or lower the hoop.' Or, 'Is *that* the best you can do?' How would you have felt?"

Daren shrugged. "Not great, I guess."

"Maybe like Gary felt yesterday?"

"But, I was just trying to get Gary to —"

"To do what he can't do yet," Mr. McCall finished. "Maybe he'll be able to dribble next year, or the year after, or maybe never. But he tried his best, just like you at seven. You didn't give him any credit for trying, did you?"

Daren knew how bad he'd have felt if his dad had made fun of him. He wouldn't have wanted to touch a basketball, not when Mr. McCall was around to watch.

"Yeah, he *did* try. And I guess I didn't give him credit for that," he finally admitted.

Daren's father peered out the window.

"Gary's in his yard," he said. "You've got time before dinner. Why not talk to him?"

Daren shook his head. "What could I say? He won't want to listen, anyway."

His father shrugged. "You'll think of something. Just try to remember what it was like to be seven."

Daren looked at his father. He thought about what the coach, Lynn, and Judy had all been saying to him. Then he got up. "Okay, I'll try."

Mr. McCall patted him on the knee. "That's my boy. Now go on downstairs and say the things Gary needs to hear."

A moment later, Daren walked into Gary's yard. Gary turned his back.

"Gary," he said. "Hey, listen, I'd really like to help you play basketball."

"Don't want to," Gary mumbled. "I can't play good."

"That's not so," Daren replied.

"I can't even bounce the ball right."

"You did okay," Daren answered.

"No, I didn't. I made dumb mistakes."

"No," Daren insisted. "You did fine. *I* made the dumb mistakes."

Gary looked at Daren. "Yeah? Really?"

"Absolutely," answered Daren. "That's why I came over. I wanted to let you know how bad I felt about giving you a hard time. You didn't deserve it. If you give me another chance, you'd be doing me a favor. What do you say?"

Gary was still suspicious. "You sure?"

Daren nodded and smiled. "Uh-huh. It won't be like yesterday. What do you say?"

Gary scuffed the ground with his sneaker. Then he looked up and smiled.

"Okay, I guess."

Daren smiled the widest smile he had all day. "All *right!* How about after my practice tomorrow?"

Gary's smile turned into a grin. "Okay."

"Fantastic!" Daren said. "See you then!"

"Yeah!" answered Gary.

As he turned for home, Daren noticed Judy watching him from her window.

In English class the next day, Daren couldn't concentrate. He wanted to clear things up with Lynn, but he hadn't been able to talk to him yet. Also, he couldn't stop worrying about practice. Would the coach walk up in front of the other Rangers and say he was off the team?

Suddenly he was aware that kids around him were giggling. He looked up to see the teacher standing over his desk, hands on hips.

"Earth to Daren. Come in, Daren," said

Ms. Cass. The giggling got louder. "If you hear me, speak or nod your head."

Daren felt his face turn red. Ms. Cass could sometimes make him feel really dumb.

"Sorry," he mumbled.

"I'm glad you could join us, Daren," said the teacher. "Now, would you do us a huge favor and answer the question I just asked?"

"I — I guess I didn't hear the question."

"I guess you didn't," said the teacher. "Sorry to break in with something as silly as English. Would you like to tell us what you were doing? I'm sure it was *terribly* important."

By now, Daren felt so tongue-tied, he couldn't have told her his name. "I, uh, no, it — sorry," he said. "I wasn't . . . um . . ."

Ms. Cass glared at him, making him more and more uncomfortable. Finally, the bell rang, ending the class and Daren's agony.

He headed for the cafeteria, trying to forget his embarrassment. Behind him, someone whispered, "Earth to Daren," and snickered. Then another voice spoke.

"She can sure be rough!" Daren was startled and happy to see Lynn beside him.

"She's just mean," said Daren. He took a deep breath. "I didn't think you'd talk to me."

Lynn grinned. "Me neither. But when Ms. C. got on your case, I took pity on you."

Daren scowled. "Why'd she do it? It's not like I cheated on a test or anything. Why did she have to make me feel like a jerk?"

Lynn shrugged. "Maybe she got mad and couldn't stop herself. You know all about *that*."

"Well, she —" Daren stopped. "Wait a second! *I* never . . . Lou and me, that's different!"

"Yeah? How?" Lynn asked innocently.

"Because *he* — I mean, *I* —"

Daren knew it was different. It *had* to be. But he couldn't think why. Was it possible that he had been as mean as Ms. Cass?

In the cafeteria, Daren saw Lou sitting by himself. Thinking back to the night before, when he had managed to smooth things over with Gary, he said, "I'm going to talk to him."

"Want me there?" Lynn asked.

"Maybe it should be just us two, okay?"

Lynn smiled. "Sounds good to me."

Lou looked up when Daren approached. "What do *you* want?" he snapped. "Can't you stop hassling me everywhere I go?"

Daren put up his hands. "I just want to —"

"Leave me alone!" Lou jumped up, knocking over his chair. Daren was stunned to see tears in Lou's eyes. "Why can't you just *leave me alone?*"

Lou rushed out of the room. Daren simply stared after him, unable to comprehend what had just happened.

Lynn came up beside him. "Well, that didn't seem to go too well," he stated. "What'd you say to him?"

Daren shook his head. "Believe it or not, I didn't even say anything to him. I didn't have the chance." He didn't tell Lynn that he thought Lou had been about to cry. But something told him that Lou had been upset before Daren had even come over. What about, Daren hadn't a clue.

When practice started that day, Daren was still a Ranger. He noticed that Lou stayed as far away from him as possible. Daren had sworn to himself that he would approach Lou to clear the air at practice, but Lou didn't give him an opening.

So instead, Daren was determined to keep his mouth shut.

The Rangers began by working on the pick-and-roll, one of basketball's basic scoring plays. Lou would plant himself at the top of the key, as if to keep defenders away from Lynn while Lynn took a jump shot. Then, as Lou broke toward the basket, Lynn would throw a pass that Lou could catch on the run and lay in for an easy two points. They ran the play over and over. At one point, Daren set himself to rebound if Lou missed his shot, and Lou slammed into him.

Daren said, "Sorry. I was out of position."

Lou stared at Daren, as if waiting for a nasty remark, then nodded. Daren saw Lynn give him a speculative look, as though he was thinking, Who is this guy, and what has he done with Daren?

Practice continued, and nobody yelled

or argued. Coach Michaels had the team work on zone defenses and backcourt traps, which he said might be useful against a powerful team like the Rebels. At least, he said, it would confuse them and make them think twice, and that could help. With Shawn playing the part of Tony Tisdale, the Rebel scoring machine, the other Rangers worked on double- and triple-teaming to make it hard for the player to get his shots up.

It was a long, hard workout, and by the end, the Rangers were totally worn out. Coach Michaels clapped his hands as the tired players grouped around him.

"Good work today. Good attitude. Keep going like this, and the Rebels are in for a surprise. See you all tomorrow."

Tired as he was, Daren felt good as he headed for his locker. He had played hard, he hadn't made anyone mad at him, and later on, he would give Gary some good tips without —

He stopped and stared at his locker door, unable to believe his eyes.

Taped to the door was an ugly cartoon drawn with a red pen. The figure in the cartoon was supposed to be him, since it had the number four on its uniform. The cartoon face had a huge open mouth full of big teeth. The caption underneath read, DAREN — BIG MOUTH, TINY BRAIN.

Lynn came up alongside him and looked at the cartoon.

"Oh, man," he said. "Not again."

Daren ripped the drawing off the locker and marched toward Lou Bettman, with Lynn alongside him. He knew he had done nothing today to deserve this. If Lou was going to pull this kind of prank, then Daren would . . . he would . . . he didn't know exactly what he was going to do, but he wanted to confront Lou with the evidence.

Lou was standing in front of his own locker, looking mad. He waved a piece of paper in Daren's face. Daren looked at it and didn't know what to say.

It was a cartoon, drawn with a red pen. The cartoon character was supposed to be Lou. It was ridiculously tall and skinny, with a big round head on top of a bony body. Tied to the cartoon player's sneakers were concrete blocks.

The caption under the cartoon read, LOU SKYWALKER — TRIPLE THREAT: CAN'T JUMP, CAN'T SHOOT, CAN'T RUN.

Before Lou could say a word, Daren showed Lou *his* cartoon.

The two Rangers exchanged long looks of amazement.

Both knew the other had been on the

court the whole practice. So neither of them had done these cartoons.

And maybe neither of them had pulled the towel or shoe prank, either.

"If it wasn't you —," Daren started.

"Then who was it?" Lou finished.

"Hey, guys," Lynn said softly, "maybe I just solved the mystery. Look over there."

He pointed to a corner of the locker room. Daren and Lou followed his finger.

Andy Higgins sat there, lettering a poster. He was using a red marking pen.

Andy was busy with his poster and hadn't seen the three Rangers watching him.

Lynn said, "I bet he did the other stuff, too: Lou's shoes and Daren's towel. Let's go over and —"

"No," said Lou. "I don't want to do that."

"You don't?" Lynn was amazed. "Why not? He's been messing around with the two of you until you were ready to fight each other. Hey, he had almost the whole *team* ready to fight! Why not let him have it?"

Lou started walking back to his locker. He looked over his shoulder at Lynn and Daren.

"Just because Andy was using a red pen, we don't know for sure that he did the other stuff. And I'm really tired of hassles. All we do lately is yell and scream. I just want to play ball and forget this garbage."

Daren said, "I feel the same way."

Lynn's jaw dropped open. "You *do?* I figured you'd want to get Andy good."

But Daren had been thinking about some of the things he had said to Andy lately. Things that he now suspected had hurt the manager's feelings. He was still bothered by what he had done to Gary, too. But he didn't want to talk about it just now.

"I'll explain it later. Right now, I just want to get out of here. I'm supposed to meet Gary Parnell and teach him some basketball."

Lynn shrugged. "Cool. You want to ride home with me?"

"You really aren't mad about what I said

yesterday? I was a total jerk," Daren admitted.

Lynn smiled. "I won't argue with you. But forget it."

Daren shook his head. "I won't forget it, but I'll try not to do it again."

Riding home, Lynn kept staring at Daren until Daren asked, "Is something wrong?"

"That's what I was going to ask you," Lynn said. "You're acting funny. You all right?"

Daren thought for a moment. "I'm not great, but I'm working on getting better."

"Whatever *that* means," said Lynn.

"It's cool," Daren replied. "I'm okay."

Gary was waiting in his driveway when Daren got home. His basketball was next to him.

He jumped up when he saw Daren coming. "Hi, Daren! Wanna watch me dribble?"

Daren smiled. "Sure, just let me put my bike away."

When Daren returned, Gary said, "Look!" He stood motionless for a moment, lifted his eyes so that he was looking over Daren's head, and started bouncing the ball. He didn't let himself look down at the ball and made four or five good dribbles before the ball got away from him.

"Great!" Daren chased the ball down and threw it back to Gary. "That's better!"

But Gary looked upset. "I was doing it even better before you got home! Really! I was really doing good!"

Daren smiled. "That's the idea. Just keep working on these things, and before you know it, you won't even have to think about it. You'll do it automatically."

"But I was really doing good before," Gary insisted. "Let me do it again!"

"Okay," Daren said. "But don't expect to get real good all at once. It takes time."

Gary wasn't paying attention. He was

staring hard at the basketball he held in both hands. Then he started dribbling again, with his eyes focused on Daren's face. After six bounces, the ball hit his foot and bounced onto the lawn. Gary looked like he might start crying.

"I was really dribbling great! I can't do it anymore!"

"Hey, hey, take it easy!" Daren reached out and patted Gary on the shoulder. "You *were* doing better. I could see. You weren't looking at the ball, and you were controlling it better."

"But I did it for a lot longer before, only you didn't see me." Gary looked miserable.

Daren sat down on the grass beside the driveway. "You're doing better than I did when I was your age. When I started trying to play b-ball, I was awful. It was embarrassing!"

"Really?" Gary looked doubtful.

"Absolutely! My dad put up a hoop for me, but I couldn't reach it. I would take that ball and *heave* it up as hard as I could, and it would hit the wall, or it wouldn't hit anything at all. Finally, Dad lowered the hoop for me — and I *still* couldn't reach it. I remember the ball hit me in the head a couple of times!"

Daren rolled his eyes, as if he'd been bonked on the head by a heavy object. Gary laughed.

"But my dad," said Daren, "he was cool about it — not like me the other day. He told me that I'd get better, and he was right."

Gary nodded. "Yeah. And *I'll* get better, too, huh?"

"Sure!" Daren stood up. "Hey, why don't we work on passing today? I bet you do better with that, because you can use both hands."

Gary frowned. "Two hands? Isn't that just for little kids?"

"No way," Daren assured him. "Even the pros make two-handed passes. I'll show you. You stand right here." He placed Gary near the garage end of the driveway and stood next to him with the ball.

"Okay. Now, hold the ball in your spread fingers, like *this*." Daren demonstrated. "When you want to pass, use your wrists and fingers to control the direction of the ball and give it speed. I'll show you."

Daren moved ten feet away and threw a gentle pass to Gary, who caught it, and grinned.

"Now you do it," Daren suggested.

Gary nodded, gritted his teeth, and threw the ball as hard as he could — straight to Daren! "Way to go!" Daren shouted. Gary's smile was huge. Daren flipped the ball back. "Let's see another one!"

Gary had no trouble getting the hang of two-handed chest passes. Daren gave him a few tips about how to position his feet and after a few minutes, held up a hand.

"Let's move on to bounce passes. They're a great way to move the ball around the court. You mix up the kind of passes you've been doing with bounce passes, and you'll keep the defense guessing. Like this."

He bounced the ball off the driveway pavement to Gary, who caught it waist-high. Gary tried getting the ball back to Daren the same way but bounced it off Daren's feet.

"Whoa!" Daren said, grinning. "Take it easy on my toes — I only have ten of them."

Gary giggled.

Daren explained how a bounce pass should be aimed to hit the floor several feet in front of the other player, so it bounces about waist-high and is easy to catch.

They practiced bounce passes and more

chest passes. Daren moved back a little bit when Gary showed he could throw the extra distance.

All the while, Daren told Gary stories about his learning to play basketball. Like how he didn't know how to tie his shoelaces when he first played and fell on his face a couple of times rather than asking other kids to help him out. Gary, who Daren had seen tie his laces, laughed. He was no longer nervous or anxious about making mistakes. He was having a great time.

Daren realized that he was enjoying himself, too.

Once, when he chased a ball onto the Parnells' lawn, he noticed that Judy was watching quietly from her porch.

After a while he forgot to notice the time. Then Judy came over and said, "Gary, it's almost time for dinner. Come in and clean up."

Gary made a face. "Just a few minutes, okay? We haven't done any shooting yet!"

"Let's leave shooting for another day, all right?" Daren said. "I had a hard practice today before I started with you, and I'm wiped out." He tossed the ball underhand to Gary, and pretended to pant, with his tongue hanging out of his mouth. "I'm not as young as I used to be."

"Okay," Gary said, with a laugh. "Next time! See you, Daren!" He sped into the house.

"I really am whipped," Daren said to Judy. "He's doing good."

"I know," said Judy. She looked embarrassed and seemed to have trouble meeting Daren's eyes with her own. "Um . . . about yesterday . . . I just wanted to say . . ."

Daren, who also felt bad about the day before, interrupted. "Hey, you don't have to . . . I mean, I wasn't . . ."

"No, really," Judy said, looking straight at Daren now, "I shouldn't have said some of the things I said yesterday, and I want you to know that I'm sorry."

"You don't have to apologize," Daren replied. "I was a jerk with Gary, and what you said was right. And what you said made me start thinking about some stuff that I should have thought about before. So let's say we're even."

Judy nodded, smiling. "Good. So, when's your next game?"

"The day after tomorrow." Daren sighed. "It's a big one, too — against the Rebels. If we lose, we may be out of the tournament this year, and those guys are really tough."

"You guys are tough, too," said Judy. "I'll come to the game and bring Gary with me."

"Yeah?" Daren grinned. "That'd be fantastic. Well, I better get inside. See you."

Judy waved. "Bye."

When Daren sat down for dinner that evening, he was starved. His father smiled, watching him clean his plate.

"Looks like you worked up a real appetite at practice," he said, offering Daren a second helping of chicken.

"Thanks," Daren said, spearing a piece. "Yeah, Coach Michaels really worked us hard, and then I was helping Gary out for a while."

Mr. McCall also took more chicken. "But it was a pretty good day, wasn't it?"

"It was a *really* good day. And maybe tomorrow is going to be even better."

Daren's mother spooned some more peas onto her plate. "By the way, Daren, how is Mrs. Bettman doing these days?" she asked. "What have you heard?"

Daren stared at her. "Huh? Hear what? I didn't hear anything!"

"Something wrong with Lou's mother?" asked Mr. McCall.

"Yes, she's very ill," replied Mrs. McCall. She looked at Daren with surprise. "You didn't know? I understand she's been in the hospital for weeks."

Daren put down his fork. He suddenly had no appetite.

Mr. McCall frowned. "Sorry to hear it. Dar, you never said that Lou's mom was sick."

Daren shook his head. "I didn't know!"

"Lou didn't tell you?" Mr. McCall asked.

"Uh-uh," answered Daren. "I don't think he told anyone."

His mother sighed. "That poor boy. It must be very hard on him."

Daren pushed back his chair. "Can I be excused?"

Mr McCall pointed to Daren's plate. "Don't you want that chicken?"

"Uh, no, I changed my mind."

Mrs. McCall gave her son a careful look. "Are you feeling all right, sweetie?"

Daren nodded. "Yeah, I just wasn't as hungry as I thought I was."

Daren trudged up to his room. He felt awful. He'd been giving Lou grief, and Lou's mom was sick! No wonder the guy was down! Why hadn't he said anything?

Daren understood that it didn't matter why. He had to get Lou to listen to him, at least long enough for him to say he was sorry.

As he and Lynn biked to school the next morning, Daren asked, "Do you know about Lou's mom?"

"What about her?"

"She's sick. She's in the hospital."

Lynn whistled. "Wow. That explains a lot. Think that's why he hasn't been playing well?"

Daren considered it. "Yeah," he said. "I bet if it was my mom or dad, my head wouldn't be in the game one hundred percent." After a minute, he added, "I could kick myself for the way I've been riding him."

"*You* didn't know his mom was sick," Lynn pointed out. "*And* you thought he was playing tricks on you."

They reached the school yard and chained their bikes to the bike rack. They were about to head into school when Daren stopped.

"Tell me something, okay?"

"Sure." Lynn looked closely at his friend.

"I just wanted to know — how come you're still my friend? I mean, the way I act sometimes, and the stuff I say to you . . . Why haven't you just walked away?"

Lynn laughed. "Believe me, it isn't easy." His face grew serious. "I just like you, I guess. You can be fun to be around, when you're not being a jerk. And we've been friends for so long, I must have just got used to you."

Daren shook his head. "I guess I'm lucky to have you as a friend."

"You better believe it!" Lynn grinned.

"Seriously!" insisted Daren. "I tried to give Gary Parnell basketball tips, but instead of helping him, I kept getting in his face. I said these terrible things, and I imitated him, made him feel really stupid. Then his sister Judy yelled at me, and I was, like, 'What did *I* do?' And the worst part was, I really didn't know!

"Then, when I thought about it, I saw that it's the same thing I do to Lou, to Andy — even *you*. And you're my best friend! When I feel bad, I want to get back by hurting someone. It doesn't really matter who."

Lynn wasn't smiling anymore. "Uh-huh. You're good at it, too."

Daren bit his lip. "I know I am. I make people feel like — like *I* felt when Ms. Cass got on me yesterday. No wonder most of the guys on the team hate me. That's why I couldn't understand why you don't hate me, too."

"You're wrong," Lynn insisted. "They don't hate you. N*obody* hates you. They're ready to be friends with you, when you show that you want to be friends with them."

Daren stared Lynn, wanting to believe him. "You think so? I don't know. . . ."

"There's one way to see for sure," Lynn said. "*Act* like a friend. When you feel yourself getting ready to give someone the needle — *stop*. I bet everyone will forget there was a problem."

"I still feel bad, especially about Lou," said Daren as they mounted the steps into school. "I'm going to talk to Lou today. I'm going to tell him I'm sorry, even if I have to hold him down to do it!"

Later that day, Daren got his chance. He and Lynn had just come into the cafeteria for lunch.

"There's Lou over there," Daren said,

pointing across the crowded room. "Maybe I can talk to him now and see what happens."

Lynn looked where Daren was pointing. "Looks like Lou is going somewhere."

Sure enough, Lou was wearing his jacket and dangling his backpack from one hand. He said something to Shawn, who was standing with him. Shawn said something back. Lou turned and hurried out of the cafeteria, practically running.

"What's going on?" Daren asked.

"Let's ask Shawn," suggested Lynn.

They crossed the room. Shawn was still watching the door that Lou had gone through, and didn't turn until Lynn said, "Hey, Shawn, what's happening?"

Shawn turned with a worried look on his face. "Hey, Lynn." Then he noticed Daren and his face went blank. He nodded, without a word.

"What's going on with Lou?" Daren asked. "Was he leaving school just now?"

The worried look returned to Shawn's face. "Yeah, he had to leave."

"How come?" asked Daren. "Is it about his mom?"

Shawn stared hard at Daren. "How do you know about his mom?"

"I — I just know, that's all," Daren replied. "Is she all right?"

"I don't know," said Shawn. "All I know is, his dad came by to pick him up and take him to the hospital."

"You knew about this, huh?" said Lynn. "Were you the only one who knew?"

Shawn nodded. "He wanted to keep it quiet. He told me because we're tight, but he made me promise not to tell anyone else. I tried to get him to let the team know, but he wouldn't."

"Boy, I sure wish I'd known earlier," muttered Daren. "I wouldn't've . . ."

He stopped, not knowing what to say.

Shawn glared at Daren. "*You* were the last person he would have told."

Daren shook his head. "Look, I know you won't believe me, but I never meant to make Lou upset. Even when I was saying all those things, I was just blowing off steam."

Shawn narrowed his eyes, but he seemed to soften a bit. "Yeah, well, I guess I'll see you guys at practice. Later."

Daren and Lynn watched him go.

"You tried, Daren, and that's the best you can do for now," Lynn said.

Daren sighed. "Hope things go better at practice today."

When Daren came into the locker room to prepare for practice, he was surprised to see

Lou at his locker, getting changed. After a moment's hesitation, he went up to the taller boy.

"How's it going?"

"Okay," Lou said, lacing up a sneaker.

Daren knew that he had to say something more, but after the way he'd behaved toward Lou, he found himself stumbling over his words.

"Listen — I — I've been doing a lot of thinking and — I'm sorry about the way I've been riding you. All I can say is that I know I was a creep and that I wish it never happened, and it won't happen again."

Lou had put on his other sneaker, but he stopped tying the laces to look at Daren. "All right. I'd rather just forget about it, myself."

Daren let out a sigh of relief. "Really? Me, too." He sat down next to Lou. "Listen, I heard about your mom. How's she doing? I saw you leave school early, and I was wondering —"

When Lou broke into a big smile, Daren suddenly realized how long it had been since he'd seen that look on Lou's face. "She's doing a lot better. Her doctor says she's going to be fine! Dad took me over so she could tell me the news herself. She'll be coming home in a week!"

"That's great!" enthused Daren, genuinely pleased for the lanky center. "It must have been tough, trying to play ball while your mom was sick."

"It was pretty bad," Lou agreed. He gave Daren a thoughtful look. "Thanks for asking about her."

Daren stood up to go to his locker but sat again quickly. He nudged Lou and pointed toward the locker room door. Andy Higgins had just come in. He saw the two Rangers looking at him and turned away quickly.

Before he could disappear, Daren called, "Hey, Andy! Come over here a second, okay?"

Andy slowly walked toward them. He looked nervous and unhappy.

"How are you doing?" asked Daren when the manager finally reached them.

"All right," mumbled Andy, looking at the floor, the ceiling, the lockers — anywhere but at Daren and Lou.

"Hey, listen," Daren said. "I know you do a lot of stuff for the team, and most of it is stuff we would hate to have to do ourselves, like picking up towels. And almost nobody ever says thank you. Well, *I* sure don't. So I figure this is a good time to say thanks."

Lou nodded. "Yeah, that goes for me, too."

Andy's mouth dropped open. "You want to — to *thank me?*"

"Right," Daren replied.

"That's about it," agreed Lou.

"It's okay," said Andy, who still looked very confused. "Um . . . I have something to say to you guys, too. I was feeling sort of, well, angry about how nobody ever appreciates the things I do around here and how some of you were always picking on me . . ."

"It wasn't right," Lou said. "We shouldn't have done that."

"I guess I was the worst one of all," added Daren. "I won't do it again."

"The thing is," Andy went on, "about those drawings and the towel and Lou's shoes being painted. I was feeling angry, I guess, and *I* was the one who —"

"Forget it," Daren interrupted.

"No big deal," said Lou.

"You mean that?" Andy asked. "Really?"

"Definitely," Lou replied. Daren nodded.

"I'll buy you new shoes," Andy offered.

"You don't have to," said Lou. "They were pretty old. I can wear them the way they are. Actually, they look cool painted red."

"Yeah, they do." Daren grinned at Lou and turned to Andy. "Where's that paint? I may paint my shoes red, too."

Lou started to laugh, and Daren and Andy joined him. Lynn and Shawn came over.

"What's up?" Lynn asked.

Lou stopped laughing and said, "We were just talking about how the Rebels are going to get totally stomped tomorrow."

"Completely," said Daren.

Shawn and Lynn exchanged puzzled looks.

"You know these guys?" Lynn asked.

"They sort of look familiar," Shawn answered. "But they sure sound different."

On the day of the game between the Rangers and the Rebels, the crowd was the biggest that Daren could remember. As he came out of the locker room into the gym, he was startled by the level of the noise. Although the game wasn't due to start for a while, almost every seat was full. He saw lots of signs scattered through the stands that said GO, RANGERS! and REBELS RULE! and similar messages. As he looked around, he happened to spot Judy Parnell, sitting with Gary. Judy noticed him and waved, and then poked Gary in the arm and pointed. Daren smiled and waved back. Gary stood up and yelled something to him, but it was too noisy for Daren to hear. He nodded to Gary anyway.

The Rangers began their warm-up drills, shooting layups. At the other end of the floor, the Rebels were doing the same thing. Daren looked them over after his first layup. Their uniforms were gray and red, and he watched their big center, Drew Capp, go up and lay the ball in. Capp was a big, strong player. It looked like he'd be able to dunk the ball someday soon. Lou Bettman was definitely going to have his work cut out for him, trying to stop this guy. Of course, the other Rangers would be there to help out.

Daren would, for sure. This was the *new* Daren. He hadn't said a nasty word to anyone and was going out of his way to be friendly. Some of the Rangers had responded immediately and been friendly, too. A few, like Shawn, were still holding back, as if they were waiting for the old Daren to put in an appearance. But so far, it hadn't happened.

Over and over during the Rangers' last practice before this game, Coach Michaels had repeated the same things: "Help each other, especially on defense. Don't be selfish on offense." Teamwork: that was the name of the game.

He had drilled the Rangers in man-to-man defense, where each Ranger guarded one opponent, and zone defense, in which each player was responsible for part of the court. He had them work on what he called their "secret weapon," a combination of zone and man-to-man in which Lynn guarded Tony Tisdale while the other four Rangers stayed in a zone defense. Everyone had worked hard, and Daren felt that the Rangers were as ready for this game as they could be.

The coach hadn't said anything to Daren about his new attitude, but there had been no further talk about benching him, either.

Coach Michaels hadn't wasted time talking about the importance of this game. He didn't have to. All the Rangers knew that, if they lost today, their season would end after the next game; they would not make the league playoffs. But if they won today, they were *in*.

Somewhere in the stands, Daren knew, were his parents, although he hadn't located them yet. His dad had taken off early from work to be here. Most of the Ranger moms and dads were here today, even the ones who, like Mr. McCall, often had to miss games because of work. Lou's dad was there, though Mrs. Bettman was still in the hospital.

Daren knew that it would really psych him up, having friends and family in the stands.

He hoped that would inspire the rest of the team to play their best, too.

Of course, he knew that the Rebels also had friends and family out there, which was probably going to inspire *them*, making the two teams even in that department.

The buzzer sounded and the teams left the floor to hear final words from their coaches before the opening tip. The Rangers grouped themselves in front of Coach Michaels. The coach had to raise his voice to be heard above the crowd.

"Remember, I want you to play a running game today. They like to play a half-court game, to walk the ball over the mid-court line and to take it easy getting back on defense. We don't want to let them do it. I think we can tire these guys out, and that we have a better bench than they do. Without Tisdale or Capp on the court, the Rebels are a different team, so let's see if we can make those two run out of gas. Look for fast-break opportunities, make them work to get the ball into their offensive zone. And watch me for defensive signals, to know when to switch from man into zone defense. You've worked hard for this one, so go out there and earn yourself a spot in the playoffs. Let's see those hands!"

The Rangers formed a circle, with all the players' hands clasped in the middle. The coach put his hand in, too. "Ready to play?"

"Yeah!" the Rangers shouted, and clapped their hands.

The Rebels controlled the ball to open the game and got it to Drew Capp. Daren moved in behind him, hands high. Capp faked a shot, then flipped a pass to Tony Tisdale, who threw in a jumper that hit nothing but net.

As Lynn grabbed the ball to put it in bounds, Daren sprinted downcourt. Lynn's inbound pass was handled by Lou, who threw it to Daren. The Rebel defense had been caught by surprise, and Daren laid in an easy two-pointer to tie the game. Daren smiled to himself. Tony Tisdale was going to have to do some serious running today to keep up with him.

The game stayed even for the first several minutes. At one point, the Rebels managed to take a three-point lead, but the Rangers came back and went up by one. Drew Capp scored a few baskets, but Lou scored as well. He threw in two fall-away jumpers that Drew couldn't block or stop. On Lou's second basket, Capp fouled him, and Lou sank the free throw.

With the score tied midway through the first half, Tony Tisdale tried to drive the lane. Daren planted himself in his path, and Tisdale rammed into him.

"That's a charge on number twelve, red!" the ref yelled. "White ball!"

The Rebels raced back on defense. They weren't going to let themselves give up any fast-break baskets if they could help it. But it looked to Daren as though Drew Capp was already beginning to pant a little.

He flipped an inbound pass to Lynn, who dribbled the ball over the midcourt line. Frank O'Malley, the Rebel point guard, picked him up. Lynn bounced a pass to Daren, who threw quickly to Peter Stuber, in off the bench. Stuber dribbled behind the key and dropped the ball off to Lynn. Meanwhile, Lou had posted himself just above the foul line.

Lynn coiled, as though he was about to launch a long jump shot. As he did, Drew moved past Lou and jumped out at Lynn. At the same moment, Lou spun and moved toward the basket. Lynn threw a high pass that Lou caught on his way up and banked in. The Rangers had taken a two-point lead on a perfect pick-and-roll.

As the Ranger fans cheered, Coach Michaels signaled for a time-out. "Looking good," he said. "Daren, Lynn, sit down and catch your breath. Shawn, Cris, you're in. Keep up the pressure! Don't let up!"

As he passed Daren, Shawn reached out his hands, palms up, and Daren slapped them. "Rangers rule!" Daren said, and Shawn grinned at him.

The Rebels managed to grab a four-point lead, but when Drew Capp and Tony Tisdale went to the bench for a breather, the Rangers came back to lead by three. Cris hit a long jump shot, and, with Drew sitting down, Lou was blocking Rebel shots and scoring inside.

It seemed to Daren that Coach Michaels had made a good prediction. Toward the end of the first half, the Rebels were looking tired, especially Tisdale, who had played most of the game.

With less than a minute left in the first half and the Rangers trailing by a point, Tony tried a jump shot. As he jumped, Daren started the fast break, running the other way. When the shot missed and bounced off the back rim, Lynn grabbed it and dribbled fast to the midcourt line. Tony Tisdale hurried back, gasping for breath, as Lynn lofted a pass to Daren. Tisdale took a running leap to block Daren's shot, but Daren pump-faked and held on to the ball. Once Tony had gone by, Daren banked in a shot off the backboard. When the buzzer sounded to end the first half, the Rangers were hanging on to a one-point lead. But they were *ahead*.

In the locker room, Andy handed out towels, drinks, and encouragement. Daren grinned at Lynn as he wiped his face.

"Tisdale will fade in the second half. He's tired now."

Lynn nodded. "Nice fake at the end, there."

"Thanks," Daren answered. "Hey, Lou!"

Lou Bettman looked over at Daren.

"Looking tough out there, big guy!"

Lou grinned. "Yo, Lynn, you're running Tisdale ragged. Keep it up!"

The coach clapped his hands to silence

the happy, excited locker room chatter. "All right, Rangers! Way to go! Now, this half, we're going to show 'em our secret weapon. Lynn, on my signal, you get in Tisdale's face and stay there, while the rest of you on court go into that four-corner zone. Tisdale may get rattled and start making mistakes. Just keep on him.

"Lou, that fall-away jumper works against Capp. Let's see more of it. I'll be making more substitutions in the second half because I want everyone as fresh as possible for the last few minutes. Don't worry about getting tired — keep playing hard. Any questions?"

Daren raised his hand. The coach pointed. "Yes, Daren?"

"I think we can get Capp into foul trouble. If you have the ball near the key, and pump like you're going to shoot, he may jump toward you. You can sort of lean in toward him, and he'll foul you. He won't be able to hold up in time."

Coach Michaels smiled. "Let's see if it'll work." He checked a clipboard. "He has one foul now. If he picks up a couple more, they'll either have to sit him down or play him with a bunch of fouls, which would handcuff him. Good idea, Daren."

Daren smiled.

"All right," called the coach, clapping his hands a few times. "Let's see the hands!"

The Rangers stuck their hands together in the middle of the circle. The coach put his in as well.

"We're going to keep running the length of the court. If you get tired, I'll put someone in for you. We're going to mix up our defenses. We're going to move the ball around on offense until someone has a really good shot. As they tire, we'll have the shots. By late second half, we'll be pulling away from them. Right?"

"Yeah!" The Rangers shouted.

"You ready to take it to 'em?"

"Yeah!" they yelled.

"Let's go get 'em!" shouted Coach Michaels.

"YEAH!" Looking determined, the Rangers ran out into the gym.

As the second half began, it was the Rebels who seemed to take control. Sam Farrell, a rugged forward, sank a long basket over Daren to give them a one-point lead. The Rebel fans yelled and waved their signs.

Lynn missed a shot, and Drew Capp nabbed the rebound. The Rebels took over, and the Rangers tried a full-court press to slow them down. Just as Tisdale finally got the ball over the midcourt line, Daren thought he saw a chance to steal. He reached in to grab the ball, and got it. And a foul, too. Lou looked furious at the call and started to protest, but Daren shook his head and hurried to the center.

"The ref's right," he said to Lou. "I hit him on the arm. My fault."

As the Rebels put the ball in play, Coach Michaels signaled for the Rangers' "secret weapon."

Tony Tisdale dribbled across the center line, and Lynn came up to cover him. The other Rangers spread out. Wherever Tisdale looked, Lynn and another Ranger stood in his way with arms outstretched. Unable to get a clear shot, he threw a pass in the general direction of Sam Farrell. But Daren picked it off. The Rangers scored on a fast break. Now it was the Ranger fans' turn to cheer.

They traded scores for several minutes, and neither team led by more than three points. Then the Rangers switched defenses, and the Rebels looked confused. With Lynn giving Tisdale fits, both on offense and defense, the star Rebel was soon breathing hard again.

Daren got a pass from Lynn inside and turned to take a jump shot. As he went up, he noticed Drew Capp leaping toward him with both hands held high. Daren leaned in as he jumped, releasing the ball just before Capp hit his shooting hand. Daren not only hit the basket but the free throw as well.

As Daren ran back on defense, Shawn stood up and clapped. "Way to go, Dar!" he yelled. A few minutes later, Cris Campbell managed to get the big Rebel center to foul again. The Rebels had no choice but to call time and put in their substitute center. With Capp out, Lou was able to get free inside for easy shots and took control of the boards. The Rangers built up an eight-point edge.

Coach Michaels gave his starters short rests, taking them out one or two at a time. The bench players, especially Peter Stuber and Shawn Howe, were fresh and kept up the defensive pressure.

Then, Tony Tisdale got a second wind and hit three straight shots. After a Ranger turnover, Rebel guard Abe Isaacs hit a jump shot from downtown — and the Rebels were within two points with a minute and a half to go. They took a time-out.

When play resumed, Drew Capp had come back off the bench. But he was one foul away from fouling out and had to be careful. Tony Tisdale finally missed one, and Lou pulled down the ball. He threw a perfect outlet pass to Lynn, who got it to Cris Campbell — and the Rangers had another fast break!

Cris found Daren on the baseline and fired a bullet pass to him. Daren got his jump shot off before Sam Farrell could reach him, and it swooshed through the net.

But Tony Tisdale completed a three-point play a few seconds later, banking in a shot from the corner and adding a free throw when Cris fouled him.

Daren looked at the clock. There were thirty seconds left, and the Rangers led by a point. Lynn put the ball in play, throwing a pass intended for Daren. Out of nowhere, Tisdale darted in front of Daren to grab the ball and lay it in.

The Rebels led!

Coach Michaels called for a Ranger time-out — their last one.

"We're going to win this with a pick-and-roll," he said, and diagrammed the play he wanted on a small chalkboard. "Let's win it!"

Lynn dribbled downcourt as the Rebels set up their defense. As the closing seconds ticked away, he passed to Daren, who fired to Cris Campbell. Lynn stayed outside, and Cris gave him the ball. Daren wheeled to the top of the key, and Lou stood in the high post, just in front of him, his back to the basket.

Ten seconds left. Daren took a quick pass from Lynn, dribbled once, and set himself for a jump shot. Sam Farrell tried to get past Lou, and Drew Capp kept his arms high to block Daren's view.

Lou spun around and darted past Drew. Daren jumped, but instead of shooting, he threw a pass that Lou caught in mid-stride. He laid it in off the glass — and the Rangers took a one-point lead, with three seconds to play!

The Rebels had no more time-outs. They inbounded the ball, and Tony Tisdale threw up a long, desperate shot, from just across the midcourt line.

It fell short. The Rangers had won!

Suddenly Daren found himself in the middle of a yelling mob of Ranger players and fans. He, Lou, and Lynn were hugging each other, and Shawn jumped on Lynn's back. Daren forced his way to the edge of the celebration, grabbed Andy Higgins, and dragged him into the middle of the crowd.

The Rangers finally started for the locker room. Daren found himself face to face with Tony Tisdale, who stuck out a hand.

"Good game," said Tony.

Daren shook hands, and replied, "Thanks. You, too."

Tisdale smiled. "We'll see you guys in the tournament."

Daren nodded as he pushed open the locker room door.

Inside, Lou was holding up his red shoes. "These shoes are good luck!" he yelled.

Shawn laughed. "Hey, let's all paint our shoes red!"

"Right!" Lynn shouted. "We'll go all the way!"

"What for?" Daren asked. "Who needs good luck . . . when you play like a *team!*"

MATT CHRISTOPHER®

THE #1 SPORTS SERIES FOR KIDS

Read them all!

- Baseball Flyhawk
- Baseball Turnaround
- The Basket Counts
- Body Check
- Catch That Pass!
- Catcher with a Glass Arm
- Catching Waves
- Center Court Sting
- Centerfield Ballhawk
- Challenge at Second Base
- The Comeback Challenge
- Comeback of the Home Run Kid
- Cool as Ice
- The Diamond Champs
- Dirt Bike Racer
- Dirt Bike Runaway
- Dive Right In
- Double Play at Short
- Face-Off
- Fairway Phenom
- Football Double Threat
- Football Fugitive
- Football Nightmare
- The Fox Steals Home
- Goalkeeper in Charge
- The Great Quarterback Switch
- Halfback Attack*
- The Hockey Machine
- Ice Magic
- Johnny Long Legs
- The Kid Who Only Hit Homers
- Lacrosse Face-Off

*Previously published as Crackerjack Halfback

Lacrosse Firestorm

Line Drive to Short**

Long-Arm Quarterback

Long Shot for Paul

Look Who's Playing First Base

Miracle at the Plate

Mountain Bike Mania

Nothin' But Net

Penalty Shot

Power Pitcher***

The Reluctant Pitcher

Return of the Home Run Kid

Run For It

Shoot for the Hoop

Shortstop from Tokyo

Skateboard Renegade

Skateboard Tough

Slam Dunk

Snowboard Champ

Snowboard Maverick

Snowboard Showdown

Soccer Duel

Soccer Halfback

Soccer Hero

Soccer Scoop

Stealing Home

The Submarine Pitch

The Team That Couldn't Lose

Tennis Ace

Tight End

Top Wing

Touchdown for Tommy

Tough to Tackle

Wingman on Ice

The Year Mom Won the Pennant

All available in paperback from Little, Brown and Company

**Previously published as Pressure Play

***Previously published as Baseball Pals